Have you ever seen a Moose brushing his teeth?

Story by Jamie McClaine
Art by April Goodman Willy

10 9 8 7 6 5 4 3 2

Library of Congress Cataloging-in-Publication Data
McClaine, Jamie
Have you ever seen a moose brushing his teeth/Jamie McClaine: illustrated by April Goodman Willy

p.cm.
Summary: Join this fun-loving moose's adventure as he learns the importance of good dental hygiene while encouraging children to do the same.
(1. Moose-Fiction. 2. Dental Hygiene. 3. Nature-Fiction.
4. Stories in rhyme-Fiction.) 1. Willy, April Goodman, ill. II Title.
LCCN: 2003102509
ISBN: 0-9709533-2-1 (Hardcover)

Printed in Canada

The illustrations in this book were executed in acrylic on sandpaper
The text type was set in Americana
Book design by Scott Willy

Printed by Friesens through Four Colour Imports, LTD., Louisville, KY

Have you ever seen a Moose brushing his teeth?
You will knee-slap and toe-tap in true disbelief.
It's a sight like no other, so it's been said
Three times a day and then right before bed.

Now why should a Moose need dental hygiene?
There's a lot more to it than shiners that gleam.
     'Cause with "toofers" like Moose's, it goes without saying
Slurping gallons of leaf juice means big time decaying!

     Armed with his toothbrush and Sparkle Moose Paste,
His Moose Floss and towelsies, there's no time to waste.
     His smile's gone lifeless and he's feeling quite low
His teeth have turned green. Oh where is their glow?

Determined and eager, he's off on his way
To care for his pearlies and stop the decay.
At break-speed he dashes 'round flowers and trees
Hurdling fences and bushes and all that he sees.

Just as the stream comes clear into view
And he's dreaming of "toofers" that look just like new,
He hears a big crash, a rustle, and BOO!
It was Ernest the Eagle from out of the blue!

Moose swerves hard to miss him, but at his great gait,
Missing Ernie the Eagle, well it was too late!
Wing and then antler; antler then wing
Rolling and tumbling, that had to sting!

Then when you thought there's no way they will stop
Untangled they were, on the stream bank they flopped.
Moose sat for a moment, then brushed himself off
Gathered paste, brush and floss and up he did hop.

He moved to the water,
his towelsies in tow
This is serious business
I want you to know.
He moved his head up
and he moved his head down
'Til the perfect reflection
was finally found.

He parted his lips
and his "toofers" escaped
With leaf juice and hay
they were thoroughly caked.
They needed some luster,
sparkle and shine
It isn't too late,
but it <u>will</u> take some time.

His favorite toothbrush with pink polka dots
His Sparkle Moose Paste he piles up on top.
He opens his mouth. He opens it wide.
On goes the paste with lots of fluoride.

He starts at the back with a slow gentle motion
Then moves to the front to start the rotation.
To the front and the back, then up and then down
All you can hear is a bristling sound.

He brushes and brushes and brushes some more
I started to wonder if his gums would be sore!
But brushing you see is his favorite thing
So much in fact that he started to sing:

"I'm a Moosey brushing away
Trying to get rid of my nasty decay.
When I began, my teeth had the slime
And that is why I am taking my time.
I brush to the left and I brush to the right
So when I'm all done I will have pearly whites!"

He brushed and he sang and the paste foam it grew
And it grew and it grew and it grew, grew, grew, grew!
Soon it had covered his great big Moose face
I think that he used too much Sparkle Moose Paste!
He shook his head hard, first to and then fro
I thought for a moment, it's starting to snow!

For the paste foam, you see, that had lathered his face
Went airborne and quickly covered the place.
I thought that would do it, he was clean in a flash
But I looked on in wonder and I heard the KER-SPLASH!

Face down in the water only antlers in view
Now came the rinsing, what was he to do?
I heard him slurp in and his slurp was a cinch
It lowered the stream by about a whole inch.

He gurgled and gargled, he rinsed then he spit
After minutes of rinsing, he finally quit.
As soon as the paste was free from his mouth,
He sat on his hiney and got the floss out.

He pulled on the string
and 'round hooves he did wind
He tugged it real tight
'til it started to bind.

Down and up went the floss,
each tooth he did hit
    Tiny leaves, hay and grass
he managed to "git."

He looked in the stream, which he used for his mirror
With his lips sealed up tight, he cautiously peered.
He started to smile, would his teeth now be white?
He covered his eyes, the glare was too bright!!!

The secret you see to avoid the tooth slime
Is to brush, rinse and floss after each Moosey mealtime.
Moose gathers his toothbrush and Sparkle Moose Paste
His Moose Floss and towelsies, he's feeling first-rate!

Down the path he is headed, he has Moose chores to do
And he knows that his brushing was long overdue!
He'll return to this spot to ward off the decay
By brushing his "toofers" at least four times a day!

Have you ever seen a Moose brushing his teeth?
You will knee-slap and toe-tap in true disbelief.
It's a sight like no other, so it's been said.
So be sure to brush after meals and before bed!

Visit the moose online at www.jafspublishing.com